PUFFIN CLASSICS

ESCAPE
TO
CHRISTMAS PAST

A Colouring-book Adventure

Illustrated by

Good Wives and Warriors

*Once upon a time
on a Christmas Eve . . .*

PUFFIN BOOKS

UK | USA | Canada | Ireland | Australia | India | New Zealand | South Africa

Puffin Books is part of the Penguin Random House group of companies
whose addresses can be found at global.penguinrandomhouse.com.

puffinbooks.com

First published 2015
Text from *A Christmas Carol* by Charles Dickens, first published 1843
Illustrations copyright © Good Wives and Warriors, 2015

001

Set in Sabon MT and Bodoni Classic Chancery
Printed in Italy
A CIP catalogue record for this book is available from the British Library

ISBN: 978–0–141–36676–0

Self contained, and solitary as an oyster.

said *Scrooge.*

Scrooge resumed his *labours*
with an improved opinion
of himself.

There was nothing at all particular about the *knocker* on the door, except that it was very *large*.

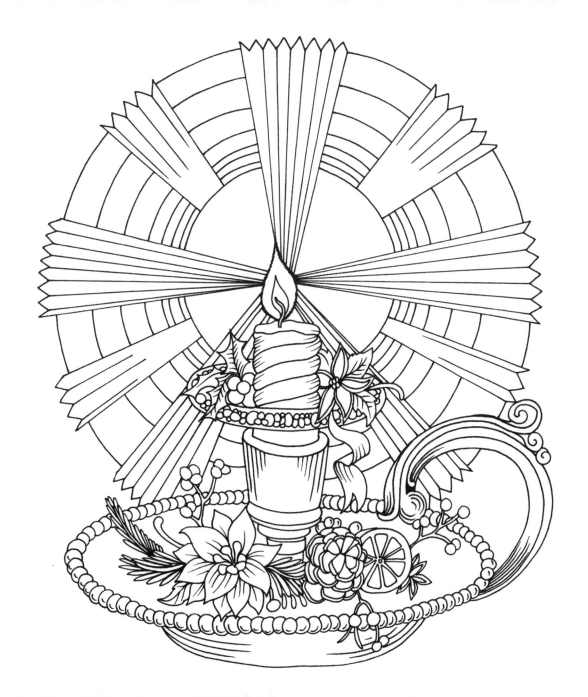

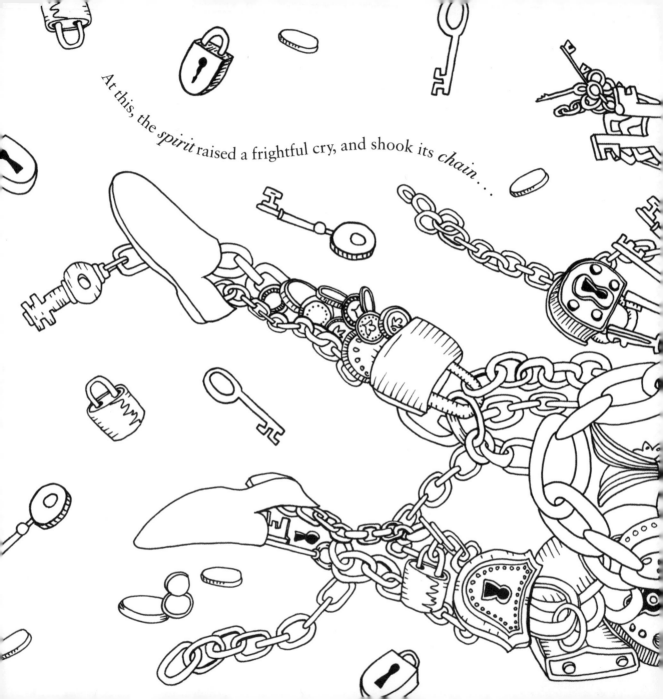

At this, the *spirit* raised a frightful cry, and shook its *chain*...

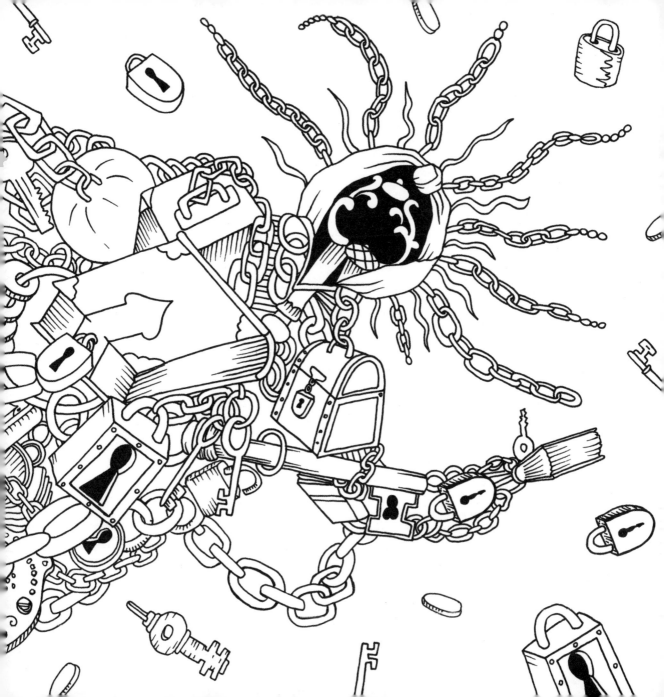

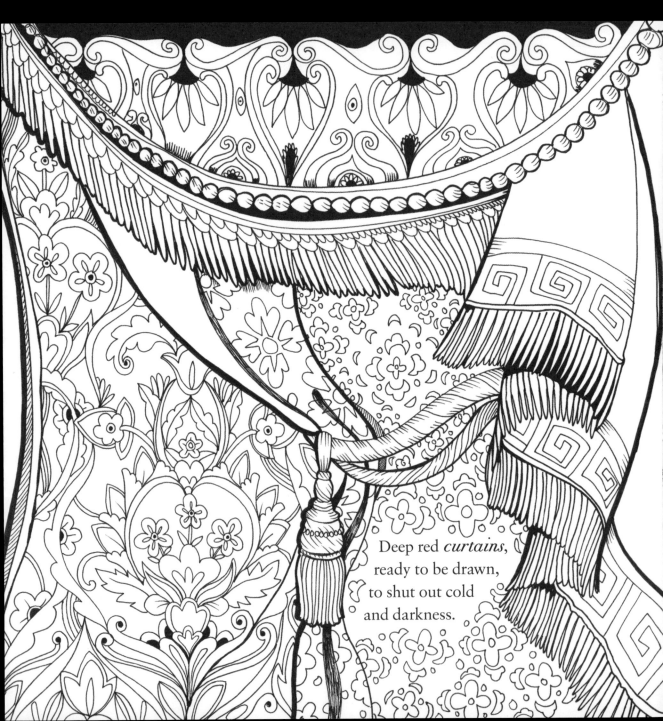

Deep red *curtains*,
ready to be drawn,
to shut out cold
and darkness.

They were now in the busy
thoroughfares of a *city* . . .

...here too it was *Christmas* time again.

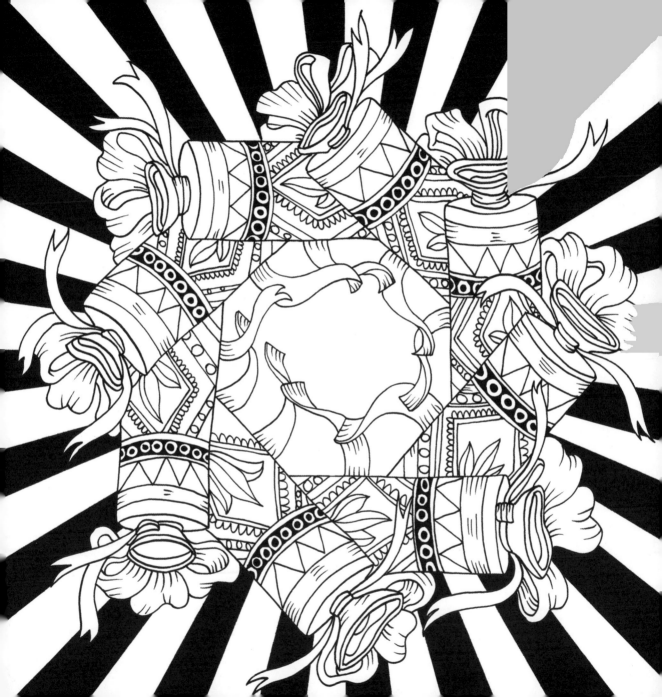

The walls and ceiling were so hung with *living green*, that it looked a perfect *grove* . . .

'I am the Ghost of *Christmas Present*,' said the Spirit.

. . . cherry-cheeked *apples*,
juicy *oranges*,
luscious *pears* . . .

Everything was good to eat and in its

Christmas dress.

. . . as if all the *chimneys* in Great Britain . . .
were *blazing* away to their dear hearts' content.

. . . the *candied fruits*
so caked and spotted
with molten sugar . . .

Such a *bustle* ensued
that you might have
thought a *goose*
the rarest of all birds.

Alas for *Tiny Tim*, he bore a little crutch . . .

Oh, a *wonderful pudding*!

Again the Ghost sped on,

above the *black*

and *heaving* sea . . .

'Ghost of the *Future*! . . . I fear you more than any *spectre* I have seen.'

'Am *I* that *man* who lay upon the bed?'
he cried, upon his knees.

Merry bells.
Oh, glorious.
Glorious!

'It's *Christmas Day*!'
said Scrooge to himself.

'It's I. Your Uncle *Scrooge*. I have come to *dinner* . . .'

'A Merry Christmas to you!'